The Curse
of Being
PHARAOH

JANICE MARRIOTT

illustrated by David Elliot

Learning Media

From the beginning of time up till last Monday, Marty was the bully and know-it-all in our class. Karen Kwon was the quiet kid at the back who no one remembered to ask to birthday parties.

But last Monday, everything changed. Now Marty sits at the back of the class, as quiet as an Egyptian mummy. Karen is giggly and happy, and for the first time ever, Mrs. Herrera had to say, "Stop talking and get on with your work, Karen."

This story is about how this big change happened.

Chapter

1

Two things were wrong when I walked into our classroom one day last week. Marty was sitting at Karen's desk writing in his math book. Karen was standing at the back of the room. She looked upset and helpless. When I stared at Karen to give her a chance to tell me what was going on, she looked away. She wasn't telling.

I wandered over to my desk, next to Karen's. Marty glared at me. He was copying her homework into his own book.

"Mrs. Herrera's not stupid," I thought. "She'll know when they both get top marks and their answers are the same."

Karen left the room. I threw my homework on Mrs. Herrera's desk and left too. I knew Marty wouldn't copy *my* work – not if he wanted to pass.

I found Karen in the library. "Why do you let him do it?" I asked.

She just smiled, a sad smile.

Marty probably knew something about her that she didn't want anyone else to know. He's always picked on the quietest kids.

"Mrs. Herrera will be there now," I said.

Karen understood. We walked back to the classroom together.

But our teacher wasn't there.

Chapter

2

Kids were standing around talking or working on the computers. Marty finished copying Karen's homework and slammed his book onto the pile on Mrs. Herrera's desk. Then he tore the homework out of Karen's book. He put the pages into the trash and threw her book across to her.

I really wanted Mrs. Herrera to come in. She'd spot what was going on in an instant, the way she always does. She would swell up like a giant hot-air balloon, rock backwards and forwards on her tiny feet, and then say, very quietly, "Marty, that is not how you behave in my classroom." And that would be that. The end. Finito.

The door opened. Great! Everyone stopped what they were doing. But it wasn't Mrs. Herrera. A tall man with a wavy smile came into the room.

He was kind of blank looking, with greenish skin. He reminded me of a long, quivering leaf with a wriggling caterpillar on it.

"I'm your teacher for the week. Mrs. Herrera is taking a course."

"I knew that," said Marty. "I read it on the staff bulletin board."

"That's real smart," said The Leaf.

So that's why Marty thought he could get away with copying Karen's work.

"We're going to do an exciting project this week," The Leaf announced.
"That is, everyone who's done their homework."
I looked at Karen.
She looked away.

Chapter

3

The Leaf got our attention by shouting and waving his arms in the air. Mrs. Herrera never shouted or waved her arms in the air. It was quite a change.

He told us he was going to teach us interesting stuff. He said we'd all get to do things, not just reading and writing.

We'd go places.

We'd make things.

We'd do drama and sport.

We were going to live our learning, he said.

It sounded OK to us.

Then he said that we were going to do a study on ancient Egypt – everything we did that week would be based on pyramids, mummies, picture writing, carving, and ancient Egyptian games.

"Cool," we said.

"Does anyone know anything about ancient Egypt?" he asked, his caterpillar smile curling and uncurling at each end.

Marty knew everything about it, of course!

"They were those people who did everything sideways with one arm up in the air. That's when they were alive. When they died, they got bandaged up tightly so that they'd fit into those enormous gold coffins."

Mrs. Herrera would have ignored Marty. But the new teacher said, "Thank you for that, Marty."

We were bored with Marty.

Marty thought he was so smart.

The Leaf showed us a picture of a hundred and seventy-two men hauling a huge statue along on a sled. And there wasn't even any snow! It was on a sandy road, and the sled had no wheels! Those ancient Egyptians were not smart.

The Leaf told us to go outside and line up in rows. We were going to pull a large stone along the ground using ropes.

We got into position. Marty was behind Karen. I watched him treading on the backs of her shoes. When she stopped, he bumped her and knocked her forwards again. The Leaf didn't notice.

Back in the classroom, The Leaf told us that had been great fun. He reckoned that two million, three hundred thousand blocks of stone were hauled into place for a pyramid. "Lucky that Karen wasn't around then," I thought.

I was going to have to watch Karen and Marty carefully because The Leaf certainly wasn't.

Chapter
4

On the second day, we made Pharaoh hats. Mrs. Herrera would have had art monitors setting out piles of things on kids' desks, and no one would have been running around grabbing other people's glue or paints or tape. The new teacher said he was into a thing called "self-expression," which we thought sounded good at first, but it ended up meaning that Marty expressed himself with a Pharaoh hat and the rest of us didn't get one finished.

Marty grabbed the pattern we were meant to cut around to make a cardboard hat. He painted the template, using all the royal blue, the color everyone wanted. Then he got the staple gun, which Mrs. Herrera never allowed anyone to touch, and shot staples into his hat. Thousands of staples so that it glittered. Then he used a whole roll of clear tape to join his hat together and make it shiny looking.

The Leaf saw that the rest of the class wasn't getting much done. This was because there was no pattern to draw round, there was no tape, and the paint table was a total mess. But he praised Marty! He said that this was what we could all achieve if we tried.

We were very bored with Marty.
Marty thought he was the new Pharaoh.

The next day, The Leaf told us this spooky
story about the pyramids. He said
that the Pharaohs were buried
in the pyramids
with all their
gold and jewels –
and servants!

"And pet cats,"
interrupted
Marty.

The Leaf said that something really terrible happened to anyone who opened the pyramid after it was sealed up. Some explorers who didn't know about the curse of the Pharaohs opened the pyramids up, and one by one the explorers died. Just before one of them stopped breathing, he screamed that an ancient Egyptian guard dog was about to eat him.

"That stuff's all superstition, for people who don't know science," said Marty.

We were sick of Marty.

Marty thought he was a star.

The next day, we did drama.

It could have been fun, but it was too disorganized. The Leaf just leaned against the wall and watched us, his curly smile wriggling on his greenish lips, while Marty took charge.

"I'll be the chief explorer person, finding the cave with the mummy and the gold and stuff in it," he said.

"You," he pointed to me, "you lie on the floor and be the mummy."

Me? What had I ever done to annoy Marty?

Chapter

5

Marty ordered Mike to take down the drapes and Bernice to take down the string line that had last week's artwork pegged on it.

There was chaos!

Bernice and Carrie stood on tables and hauled the string down. Paintings crashed everywhere. A team of tomb builders piled up chairs and desks to make the Pharaoh's tomb. Then Mike tugged the drapes off the curtain pole, and they slid down in a cloud of dust. As they fell, they knocked everything off the shelf onto the floor. It was like a rock slide in an ancient Egyptian quarry.

"Now," shrieked Marty, "we need that mummy!"

I took a step backwards, but unfortunately I stood on Lulu's painting. She pulled. It ripped.

She lunged at me.

"You!" Marty shouted to me. "Get in the tomb and lie down."

Just then Mike staggered up with the two long, dusty drapes hanging from his arms and head.

"Aaaaaatishooooooo!" sneezed Kyle, who had hay fever.

I started to crawl under the chair legs, but it was too late. Marty had another plan.

"Wait!" he called again. "You've got to be mummified first."

I looked over the mess and chaos at The Leaf. But he was still just standing there with a dull green glow in his eyes and that caterpillar smile on his lips.

Mike had to cover me in the drapes, and Carrie tied the string around so that I looked like a bundle. Then Marty pushed and kicked me into position between the chair legs, among the balls of fluff and dust.

Marty decided he needed all the rest of the class to be diggers. This meant that everyone had to move the chairs around all the time. I don't mind telling you, I was scared. Any moment now a table or chair was going to fall on top of me. And I couldn't move. Something very bad was going to happen. I just knew it!

Chapter

6

What did happen was that the bell rang.

Everyone stopped, looked at The Leaf, looked at the mess, and then ran out of the room. Everyone except Karen, who was sitting at the back of the room doing extra math homework, and me, bundled up under a mound of chairs.

The Leaf looked at the jumble. He ran his fingers through his hair and went off to the staff room.

Karen got on all fours and untied me. She was helping me out from under the pile of chairs when the door was flung open and someone strode into the room. All we could see were two large, shiny boots.

"What's going on?"

It was a roar, an explosion almost. It was Mr. Kusnetzov from room four, and he was very, very angry. Karen and I had to clean everything up. After break, the rest of the class went in with Mr. Kusnetzov's class for singing, but Karen and I had to keep on cleaning. The Leaf wasn't around.

In the afternoon we did math, like a normal day. Another teacher was in the room with us while The Leaf did the teaching. Marty said he couldn't work because the sun was shining too brightly. We couldn't close the drapes. There were no drapes.

The next day, The Leaf was back, teaching us by himself. He told us to make pyramids for math. No instructions. We had to work it out for ourselves. "Use anything you like," he said.

Most people stuck to cardboard, and "stuck to" is what we did. If you've tried gluing one side of a pyramid to another, you'll know that the Pharaoh's curse is still working.

Karen had this great idea to make her pyramid out of Lego. We went to the Lego box and started getting the bits we needed. We got a green base plate and handfuls of yellow blocks and put them into a carton. Back at our table, Karen started working out the lengths of the walls and how tall our pyramid would be. I was stirring the blocks around in the carton, looking for some small ones to make the top, when I felt someone there beside me. It was Marty.

Chapter

7

Without a word, Marty took the carton from me and walked away.

I went after him and tried to take the carton back. The Leaf looked up from a book he was reading and asked me to leave Marty alone.

"You have to learn to share and work together when you make things," he said. "You are a team."

After that, Karen and I spent math time drawing horses and spaceships and just messing about.

At the end of math, The Leaf asked Marty to show off his Lego pyramid, complete with a door that opened and a spaceman lying down inside.

No one in the class was interested.

Marty thought he was a superstar.

We were all glad when the bell rang and the weekend started.

After the weekend, on that fateful Monday, I caught Marty looking in Karen's bag in the cloakroom before class. We were fighting when in through the cloakroom door came – a Pharaoh from ancient Egypt!

We both froze. There in front of us was this ghost! It had huge black hair that looked like a side panel off a car, and it was wearing a long white robe thing. Neither of us could move. I suddenly thought about the Pharaohs coming back to haunt people.

Chapter 8

The Pharaoh lifted up a hefty arm covered in bracelets and hair. I was about to be zapped by an ancient Egyptian! I clutched at Marty.

The Pharaoh took his hair off!

"Hey, sorry, guys," said the Pharaoh, otherwise known as The Leaf.

I still couldn't speak. I was trembling, but Marty said he wasn't at all scared. He could tell immediately, he reckoned, that the jewels were fake.

"I'm never scared," he said, "because I know how the world works."

"That's great," smiled The Leaf. "I thought we could all dress up today."

I felt a total jerk.

Marty thought he was a megastar.

In the classroom, The Leaf put us in pairs. Even though he was always talking about personal freedom, he didn't let us choose our own pair. He put boys with girls. There was heaps of squawking and fuss. In the chaos, I couldn't stop Marty being paired up with Karen.

The Leaf dropped a huge sack of toilet rolls on the floor.

"I'm not dressing up in that!" said Zelda.

"Everyone's either making or being a mummy," he said.

The Leaf told us we had to choose who would be the mummy and who would do the bandaging. There was a lot more squawking and fuss.

Of course, with Marty and Karen, there was no contest. He said that the top people, the Pharaohs, were turned into mummies and the bandaging people were slaves. So, obviously, he had to be the mummy.

Karen looked across at me for the first time, and she smiled – a big smile. I could tell she had a plan.

She started bandaging.

Chapter 9

Now the thing about Karen is that she always does things properly. She always writes the best and longest stories. Her math is always the neatest. She bandaged thoroughly!

Marty complained about the soft, pink toilet rolls she was using. So she swapped with me and started bandaging round his chest and arms with natural, recycled paper.

"Not recycled! I'm not having used toilet paper wrapped around me!"

Karen swapped the natural for a white economy pack of maximum strength.

Marty told anyone who'd listen that he knew the real way the Egyptians did their bandaging. The arms got bandaged across the chest. So Karen folded his arms over his chest and carried on.

"Hey! I need to scratch my nose!"

That was the first thing Marty said that showed us he was trapped. Karen took no notice – she just went right on bandaging.

My paper fell down around my mummy's ankles, and Suzi giggled and told me to stop – so we stopped. Soon everyone had stopped – everyone except Karen. We all watched Karen as she went round and round Marty.

She sat down and rolled layer after layer around his legs. She had this serious look on her face.

Marty couldn't do a thing about it. His face went pink. I guess he was beginning to realize just how lucky the Pharaohs were – they were dead when they had this done to them!

"I've got to scratch an itch!" Marty whined. You could tell by the way he was wriggling that he was trying to get out. But he couldn't move.

Chapter 10

"I'm getting hot," Marty whimpered. "I've got spots in front of my eyes."

Marty's face was going white, like the paper. We kept encouraging him by telling him about the photographer who was coming that afternoon to take a photo for the local paper.

"You'll be a hyper-mega-superstar Pharaoh, Marty."

"I forgot!" yelled The Leaf. He left the classroom to phone the photographer and ask him to come after school that afternoon.

Marty's face went from white to pale green. We propped him in a corner because he was no longer able to stand upright.

"I'z zz-see zz-spots," he mumbled.

"Those are the spots on the Pharaoh's guard dog. Look out!" I shouted.

Marty moaned strange sounds. We stuck his Pharaoh hat on his head. Then the bell rang for lunch.

Everyone left. Karen and I were last. We planned to shut the door behind us, leaving the mess, with the mummy propped in the corner like a huge baseball bat.

"What is all this mess?"

I knew that voice. It was Mrs. Herrera, back from her course. She stood there, puffing herself up, ready to explode.

"The teacher's just gone to get a photographer," I whispered.

"There will be no photographers here, thank you," she said, looking around at the toilet paper all over the floor.

"What sort of work have you done this week?" she asked quietly.

"We didn't learn much," I said.

"Get rid of that rolled-up thing in the corner, please."

The thing in the corner moaned, trembled, and slid to the floor. Mrs. Herrera looked stunned. Then she walked up to the Marty mummy.

"If I'm not mistaken, that's Marty Miller in there."

We loosened some of the toilet paper and peered at him.

Would Mrs. Herrera think that Karen and I had beaten Marty up? Would we have to go to the principal? Would letters be sent home? I didn't dare look at her.

"I think," she said slowly, looking straight into Marty's eyes, "that maybe one child in this class has learned something this week."